This book belongs to

· ·

To my daughter Anyaugo, who loves chickens,
adventure and meeting interesting people.
Nnedi

To my loving grandmother Banoo.
Mehrdokht

American edition published in 2017 by Lantana Publishing Ltd.
www.lantanapublishing.com

First published in the United Kingdom in 2015 by
Lantana Publishing Ltd., London.
info@lantanapublishing.com

Text © Nnedi Okorafor 2017
Illustration © Mehrdokht Amini 2017

The moral rights of the author and illustrator have been asserted.

Distributed in the United States and Canada by Lerner Publishing Group, Inc.
241 First Avenue North
Minneapolis, MN 55401 USA

For reading levels and more information, look for this title at
www.lernerbooks.com.

Printed and bound in Hong Kong.
Cataloguing-in-Publication Data Available.

ISBN-13: 978-1-911373-15-5
eBook ISBN: 978-1-911373-05-6

Chicken
in the
Kitchen

Nnedi Okorafor • Mehrdokht Amini

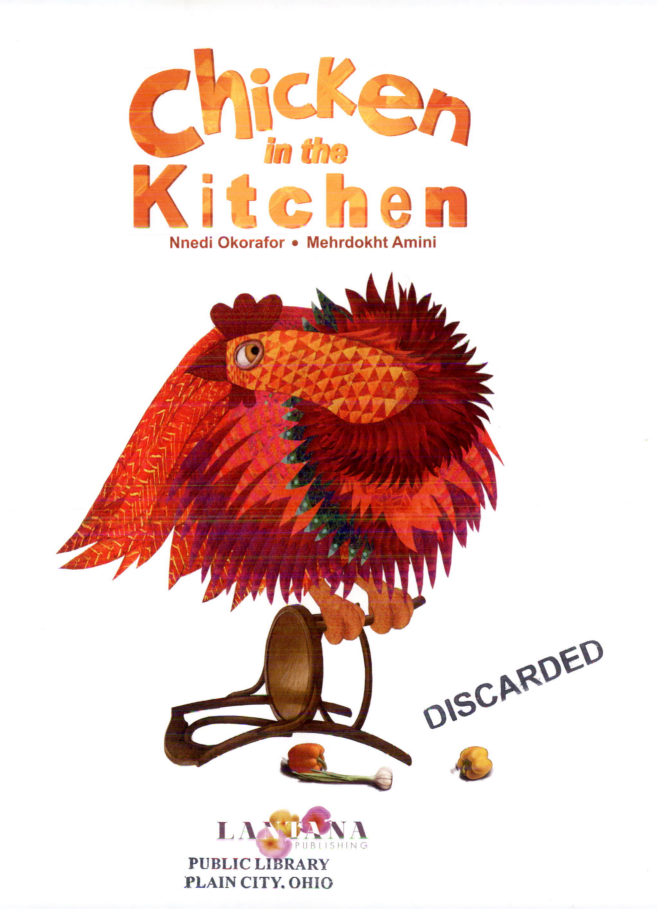

LANTANA PUBLISHING

It was late at night.
A noise had woken Anyaugo.

She climbed out of bed and crept
quietly towards the kitchen.

"Oh my!!" Anyaugo whispered.

What was she going to do? There was a giant chicken in the kitchen! It was going to spoil the food her mother and aunties had cooked for the New Yam Festival the next day.

She *had* to do something!

"Buck buck peh-CUCK!" said the chicken happily.

The New Yam Festival marked the beginning of the harvest season. It was a time for being thankful, dancing, seeing friends and family and, of course, eating lots of yams.

Anyaugo couldn't let the chicken ruin the yam dishes in the fridge!

What is wrong with it? Anyaugo wondered.
The chicken was causing a lot of mischief!
Anyaugo wished she knew where her friend
the Wood Wit was. He was a nature spirit.
He would know what to do.

Anyaugo tried to muster up some courage.

I'm going to just…tell it to leave!

Or maybe not!

It was time to get help from the Wood Wit.

Where is it? Anyaugo wondered.

The Wood Wit could travel
through anything made of wood.
It could be almost anywhere.

Maybe it was playing outside
in the coconut trees? If so, she
would never be able to find it.

"Are you in there?"
Anyaugo called.

"*There* you are," Anyaugo said.

"There *you* are," the Wood Wit said. It laughed. "You have a chicken in your kitchen and you want to get rid of it."

"How do you know?"

"I know everything that the wood knows," the Wood Wit said.

Anyaugo didn't understand what the Wood Wit meant, but that didn't matter. The Wood Wit was always saying odd things like that.

"Will you help me?"

"Sure. I *love* being helpful…"

"It looks quite annoyed," the Wood Wit said. "Whatever have you done to it?"

"I didn't do anything!" Anyaugo insisted. "How can I make it leave?"

"Ask it," the Wood Wit said. "But ask it in Chickenese."

"But I don't speak Chickenese!" cried Anyaugo.

"Say 'buck buck CLUCK,'" the Wood Wit suggested. "But you have to say it *just right*!" It burst out laughing, amused with itself.

Anyaugo lifted her chin, clenched her fists and said…

The chicken flashed the sunniest, shiniest, sweetest smile Anyaugo had ever seen!

Then the Wood Wit began to hum. It sounded like three voices and a soft drumbeat. It was with the sound of the drumbeat that Anyaugo understood.

How had she not guessed it? This was *more* than a chicken!

"Buck buck?" it said softly.
It was asking her to dance!

Later that night, when Anyaugo finally went to bed, she smiled to herself.

Her father had told her about the powerful masquerade spirits that came to participate in the New Yam Festival.

Masquerades visited the community during festivals, ceremonies and events. Some were spirits of the elements, like the land and water. Others were ancestors returning to dance, showing that death was a natural part of life.

This one must have come for a midnight snack!

At the New Yam Festival the next day,
Anyaugo ate several yam dishes and saw
some of the biggest yams she had ever seen.

But though she watched many wonderful masquerades perform, she did not see the chicken masquerade among them. *Until...*

**If you enjoyed this book,
why not try other picture books by**

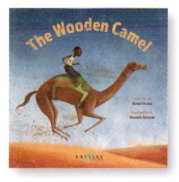

Lantana Publishing is an independent
publishing house producing award-winning
children's books by authors and illustrators
from around the world.

*Because all children
deserve to see themselves
in the books they read.*